This book belongs to:

_____

_____

_____

_____

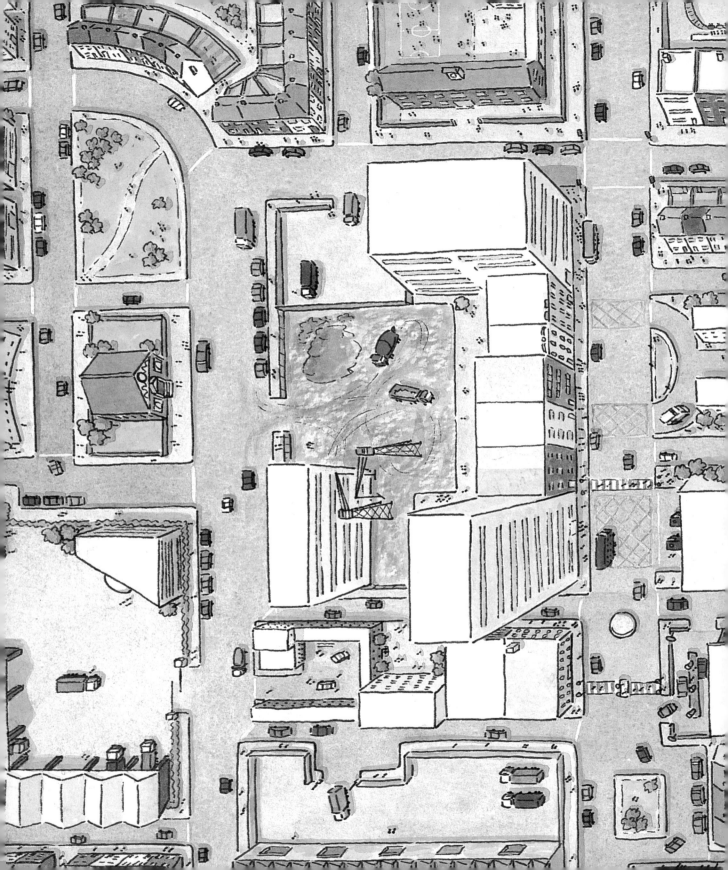

Steady Eddie and RoSPA
working together to improve road safety awareness.
To make a donation to RoSPA, please write to the
Fundraising Manager,
The Royal Society for the Prevention of Accidents,
Edgbaston Park, 353 Bristol Road, Birmingham B5 7ST.

LITTLE TIGER PRESS
An imprint of Magi Publications
22 Manchester Street, London W1M 5PG
First published in Great Britain 1999
Text and illustrations © Little Tiger Press
Text by Linda Jennings
Illustrations by Sami Sweeten
Based on characters and stories by Illtyd Barrie Thomas
Steady Eddie is a registered trademark
of Stobart Management Services
Printed in Singapore • All rights reserved
ISBN 1 84143 000 5
1 3 5 7 9 10 8 6 4 2

STEADY EDDIE
on Safari

LITTLE TIGER PRESS
London

Steady Eddie was going to Treetops Safari
Park to deliver animal feed.
"Lucky you!" said Lorretta Lorry enviously.
"I've always wanted to see a lion."
Lorretta liked a bit of excitement. She
sometimes felt she had all the boring jobs.

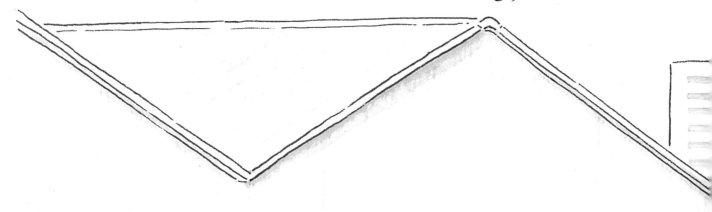

"There's no time to stand around talking," said Mr Overall, the Depot Manager, bossily. "You've got lots of jobs to do. Off you go now, Steady Eddie."
With a big sigh, Lorretta watched Steady Eddie drive out of the depot with his load.

Steady Eddie wasn't far out of town when his
friend, Jock the Tartan Tanker, drew up beside
him. He was looking very smart and gleaming.
"I'm on my way to the Truck Show," said Jock.
"Everyone who is *anyone* will be there. How
do I look?"

Steady Eddie noticed a splash of mud on Jock's side. The big tanker was very vain. If he saw the mud he'd probably drive back to his depot for a wash. Then he would miss the Truck Show altogether! "You look absolutely fine!" Steady Eddie assured him.

When Steady Eddie finally arrived at the entrance to Treetops Safari Park he was surprised to see Jock again, parked on the grass verge.
"Why Jock, what are *you* doing here?" asked Steady Eddie.

"Can't you see that traffic jam? I'll never get to the Truck Show if I'm stuck behind it," complained Jock. "Hey, I could take a short cut through the Safari Park."
"I don't know about that," said Steady Eddie. "You'll have to ask the keeper first. He wouldn't want you to scare the animals."

Steady Eddie drove on ahead, without waiting to see if Jock was following him. He hadn't gone far before THUD! something jumped on to the roof of his cab! and BUMP! something else landed beside it!

"It's the chimpanzees!" groaned Steady Eddie, as a third chimp banged on the window. "Come on you guys, enough's enough. I've got work to do!"

The chimps knew that if they didn't let Steady
Eddie drive on, they wouldn't get any food so,
one by one, they dropped from the lorry and
scampered away through the grass.
Steady Eddie hadn't gone far before he had
to stop again . . .

. . . because Max the Lion was fast asleep in the middle of the drive! Very, very carefully, Steady Eddie drove round him. Max didn't so much as twitch a whisker! "Wouldn't Lorretta have loved to see that lion," thought Steady Eddie.

When Steady Eddie unloaded at the main building, Ken the Keeper discovered that the monkey nuts were missing. Quickly, he got on the phone to Mr Overall. "Yes, we need them today, we've run out completely," said Ken.

Ken put down the phone. "All sorted out," he said. "They're sending some over with Lorretta Lorry."
Steady Eddie smiled to himself. Wouldn't Lorretta be thrilled!

In the meantime, Jock had sneaked into the
park while the keeper's back was turned.
"This will save me lots of time," he chuckled.
"How clever of me to think of it!"

Jock drove on, but he didn't get far. THUMP! went something on his roof, and THUD! as something else joined it. You've guessed it! The chimps were back!

The chimps had never seen a tartan lorry
before. They loved it. One danced a jig on
the roof, while another playfully tugged at
Jock's ginger beard. A third pressed Jock's
horn and tooted it loudly.

Jock liked playing jokes himself,
but he didn't like what those chimps
were doing to him!
"GET OFF!" he screamed. "Scram!"

At last the chimps jumped from the tanker and ran off into the bushes, but not before one of them had left a big, deep scratch right across Jock's gleaming tartan paintwork.

Jock drove on. Half way across the park a baby elephant squirted him with dirty water. Jock looked a real mess. He didn't even know if he wanted to go to the Truck Show now. But, just as he thought his troubles were over . . .

. . . he came across Max the Lion still
sleeping, bang in the middle of the road!
Jock often liked to make people jump by
honking his horn. He thought this trick
would work very well on Max.
HONK! HONK! he went and . . .

GRRRR! snarled Max, leaping to his feet and thrusting his head through Jock's open window. What a nasty set of teeth! All Jock's usual bravado suddenly left him. "Help me!" he quivered.

Steady Eddie and Lorretta Lorry arrived
on the scene at the same time.
All the animals loved Steady Eddie, so he
was able to persuade Max to stop growling.
"Nice lion," said Jock, putting on a brave
face, as Max gave him a big, sloppy lick.

"You shouldn't have left your window open," said Steady Eddie. "Every visitor knows that. But then you weren't a real visitor, were you?"

"Er-no," said Jock, his red tartan paintwork blushing an even deeper red.

Lorretta Lorry was thrilled to bits. Here she was in Treetops Safari Park, face to face with a real lion! Then, feeling sorry for Jock, she said, "I wonder if Jock will make it to the Truck Show."

"I think he's had enough excitement for one day," laughed Steady Eddie. "It's my guess he's on his way back home for a good wash and brush up."

And so he was – but not without a final surprise!

STEADY EDDIE

I have learned all about road safety. It is very important that you learn all these tips too.

1   Always stop, look and listen before crossing the road. This means stop at the kerb, look for vehicles and listen for sounds of traffic that you may not be able to see coming. When it is safe, you can step off the kerb and cross the road.

2   Try to cross a road with a grown-up you know. Hold their hand while crossing.

3   **Never** run straight across a zebra crossing. Sometimes vehicles are going too fast to stop. Always step carefully on to the crossing when you are sure there is no traffic coming.

4   You must always **walk**, never run, across a road. If you **run** you are more likely to **fall**.

5   Always find a **safe place to play**, away from the road.

6   Never cross the road on a corner, the brow of a hill or, if you can help it, between **parked cars**. This is because the driver may not be able to see you and you may not see them.

7   Always **wait** at a pedestrian crossing until the **green person** lights up and you have checked that the **road is clear**. Never cross when the red person is lit up even if you can't see any vehicles approaching.

8   Always wear bright clothing to help the drivers see you, especially in winter when it is dark.

9   Never cross a busy main road unless you can cross safely by using a **pedestrian crossing**, a **zebra crossing**, a **footbridge**, a **subway** or at the **traffic lights**. Make sure that you **know where these safe places are** in the area you live.

10   **Keep safe at all times**. Always tell someone where you are going. Never talk to anyone you **don't know**.

Join the LITTLE TIGER CLUB now for lots more books to enjoy!

Schools can join too and will receive a special enrolment pack.

How to be a Happy Hippo
JONATHAN SHIPTON & SALLY PERCY

BABY SEAL ALL ALONE
Linda Cornwell
Gavin Rowe

The Very Noisy Night
Diana Hendry
illustrated by Jane Chapman

Little Tiger's big surprise!
Julie Sykes · Tim Warnes

STEADY EDDIE Foils the Plot

The Very Lazy Ladybird
Isobel Finn & Jack Tickle

Join the LITTLE TIGER CLUB now and receive a special Little Tiger goody bag containing badges, pencils and more! Once you become a member you will be sent details of special offers, competitions and news of new books. Why not write a book review? The best reviews will be published on book covers or in the Little Tiger Press catalogue.

The LITTLE TIGER CLUB is free to join. Members can cancel their membership at any time, and are under no obligation to purchase any books. If you would like details of the Little Tiger Club, please contact: Little Tiger Press, 22 Manchester Street, London W1M 5PG, UK. Telephone: 0171 486 0925, Fax: 0171 486 0926
Visit our website at: www.littletiger.okukbooks.com